Sarah and Jessica are going to New Zealand for a holiday.
They are very excited.

Jessica is near the window. 'Look!' she says, 'There's
Auckland! We're here!'

'But we're late,' Sarah answers. 'When's our bus?'

'At one o'clock,' Jessica says. 'We can get a taxi from the
airport to the bus station.'

At the airport, the girls look for a taxi.

'Look!' Jessica says. 'That boy's waving to us!'

'Excuse me! Are you late?' the boy calls to them. 'Do you want this taxi? I can wait.'

'Thank you very much!' the girls answer.

'To the bus station, please,' Sarah says to the driver.

She smiles at the boy and they drive away.

The taxi stops at the bus station. Suddenly, Jessica sees a
mobile phone on the taxi floor.

'Is that your mobile phone?' she asks the driver.

He looks at it. 'No,' he answers. 'It's the boy's mobile.'

Sarah takes it. 'Perhaps I can find his address,' she says. 'Yes!
His name's Michael. Tomorrow he's at Ninety Mile Beach.
We can give it to him there.'

The girls wait at Ninety Mile Beach. They eat and watch
the buses. The buses aren't driving on a road – they are
driving on the long beach.

'Look for Michael!' Jessica says. But Sarah is looking at
the sea.

Suddenly, Jessica sees him. 'He's on that bus!' she says.
She waves. Michael waves to her, but the bus doesn't stop.

4

The girls get on a bus.

'Can we catch him?' Jessica asks.

'I don't know,' Sarah answers. 'I can't see his bus now.'

Suddenly, they hear a *beep*. Sarah looks at the mobile.

'There's a message for Michael,' she says. She reads the message. 'It's important,' she says. 'Perhaps we can find him tomorrow at the Sky Tower in Auckland.'

At the Sky Tower, the girls can't see Michael.

'He isn't here,' Sarah says. A woman bungy jumps from
the tower. 'I can do that,' she says. 'Are you coming,
Jessica?'

'No,' Jessica answers. 'But I can watch you from here.'

'Please watch my bag too,' Sarah says. She gives her bag
to Jessica and she goes up the tower.

Sarah jumps. It is a very long jump. She comes down near the street and she sees Michael.

Jessica sees him too. 'Michael! Come back! We've got your mobile!' she calls to him. But Michael is walking away.

She runs after him. She doesn't take Sarah's bag.

'Jessica! My bag!' Sarah calls.

Jessica and Sarah are very unhappy. They can't find
Michael and they can't find Sarah's bag. Sarah has no
money now.

'Sorry,' Jessica says. 'But I've got some money – and we've
got tickets for the Glow-worm Caves.'

'OK. Let's go there tomorrow,' Sarah says. 'Michael is going
too. We can look for him there.'

The girls go on a boat into the dark cave. The lights from the glow-worms are very beautiful and it is very quiet. Suddenly, there is a *beep* from Michael's mobile. The lights go dark.

The people in the boat are angry. 'No mobiles!' they say.

'We're very sorry,' Sarah says. She sees a new message for Michael. 'Perhaps we can find him in Rotorua.'

'Rotorua is very interesting,' Jessica says. 'I like the hot water.'

'Yes,' Sarah answers, 'but I can't see Michael.'

'Where is he tomorrow?' Jessica asks.

Sarah looks at the mobile. 'He's in the South Island,' she says. 'The boat's very expensive. Can we go?'

'Yes,' Jessica says. 'I've got money for the tickets.'

Sarah and Jessica take a boat to the South Island. It is very cold, but the café is expensive. Suddenly, there is a *beep* from Michael's mobile phone.

'Oh, no! Not again!' Sarah says. She reads the message. 'Michael's mother and father are worrying about him, and we can't find him. Let's take his mobile phone to the police station in Kaikoura.'

The girls take the mobile phone to the police station.

Then they go down to the sea.

'Let's go and see the whales,' Jessica says.

'We can't,' Sarah answers. 'The tickets are expensive.'

Suddenly, Jessica sees Michael. She runs to him.

'Your mobile's at the police station,' she says, 'and you've got messages from home.'

Michael quickly calls home. He smiles. 'My mother and father are well,' he says, 'and they've got £100,000 from the lottery! They're sending some money to me for my holiday. Now I can give you a surprise.'

'What surprise?' Jessica asks.

'Wait and see,' Michael says. He walks to the Whale Watch ticket office.

'Thank you for my mobile,' Michael says to the girls.

'Thank you for the surprise!' Jessica says. She is very excited.

'Do you like the whales?' Michael asks.

'I love them!' Jessica answers. 'They're beautiful.'

'Yes, and New Zealand is beautiful too,' Sarah says.

'This is an adventure!'

ACTIVITIES

Before you read

1 Look at the pictures in the book. Talk to a friend about the story. What do you think?

    a Why are the girls in New Zealand?

    b Who do they meet? Where do they meet him?

    c Do they have any problems?

2 Look at the Word List at the back of the book. What are the words in your language?

3 What do you know about New Zealand? Are the sentences right or wrong?

    a New Zealand is near France.

    b New Zealand is an island.

    c Auckland is an important town in New Zealand.

    d There are 2,000,000 people in New Zealand.

While you read

4 Answer the questions.

    a Who sees Auckland first? ....

    b Who sees Michael's mobile in the taxi? ....

    c Who bungy jumps from the Sky Tower? ....

    d Who has no money? ....

    e How much is a Whale Watch ticket? ....

    f How much money do Michael's mother and father get from the lottery? ....

    g Who buys the Whale Watch tickets? ....

15

5 Read the story again. Where do Jessica and Sarah start their holiday? Then where do they go?

After you read

6 Work with a friend.

Student A: You are Jessica. Telephone your mother or father. Talk about your holiday.

Student B: You are Jessica's mother or father. Answer the telephone. Ask questions.

7 After the Whale Watch, Michael sends a message to his mother from his mobile. Write the message.

8 Jessica and Sarah love New Zealand. What country do you like? Write about it.

Answers for the activities in this book are available from the Penguin Readers website. A free Activity Worksheet is also available from the website. Activity Worksheets are part of the Penguin Teacher Support Programme, which also includes Progress Tests and Graded Reader guidelines. For more information, please visit:
www.penguinreaders.com.